Felicity Fox

by Alia Einstein Diez

illustrated by Shanti Ghosh

Felicity was so excited! Her mama gave her a wonderful birthday present and she couldn't wait to try it out! The little foxling ran outside, down the hill and sat by the stream next to several large stones. She took a box of colored chalk pieces out of her nap sack.

Felicity stared at her gift for a moment happily, took out a piece of chalk and started drawing. She drew the sun, trees, flowers and her favorite thing in the world - a rainbow.

"Oh, the colors look so beautiful!" She exclaimed to herself joyfully.

A small head popped out from behind one of the rocks. "What looks so beautiful?" asked Wesley Weasel.

"Oh! you startled me!" shrieked Felicity, jumping up in fright her chalk pieces flying all around her.

"Sorry," Wesley muttered as he came around the stone to look at the drawings. "Nice colors! Can I try?"

Felicity held on tighter to the chalk in her hand and pinched her lips tightly. She did not want to share her precious birthday gift with anyone, especially since her mama gave the chalk to her a moment ago and she was only just starting to play with them.

"Aw, come on, Felicity, I only want to try one. Pleeeease?" Wesley begged.

"Alright," Felicity mumbled half-heartedly.
"Great!" Wesley squealed and grabbed a piece of chalk on the ground.

"Ooooooo this is lovely! I'll add some clouds over here."
"Don't ruin my picture!" protested Felicity.

But Wesley wasn't listening and he grabbed another piece of chalk and started coloring all over Felicity's drawings.
Tears started streaming out of her eyes and she started collecting the chalk and putting them back in the box.
"I need to go home. Give me back my colors!" she demanded.

Wesley returned a piece
of chalk to Felicity, and bounced behind the rock where he had come from with a quick "goodbye!"

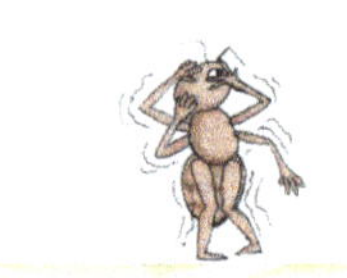

Before she could reply, Felicity looked up and he was gone. She collected the rest of the chalk and carefully put them back in the box. That is when she noticed that one piece was missing.

"Oh no!" she exclaimed.

She searched around every stone, but the piece was gone. She looked behind the rock that Wesley had come from and noticed a hole in the ground.

"I suppose that is his home" she said dejectedly.

When Felicity got home, she ran to her mother with tears pouring down her cheeks and told her what happened. "That horrible weasel took my favorite color! Orange, like my fur" she wailed.

Felicity was so distraught that she didn't even notice her grandpa was sitting on his favorite rocking chair, observing the whole scene. "Come here, lovey. I want to tell you a story" he said sweetly.

"A story? Now grandpa?" Felicity stammered perplexed. "Yes dear. I think it will do you good to hear it" he smiled and patted his lap for his granddaughter to sit on it. She did so and looked quizzically into the old fox's kind, wise eyes.

"A long time ago, when I was your age" he started, "my grand-daddy had a beautiful gramophone."

"What is a gramophone, grandpa?" Felicity inquired. He chuckled and said "a gramophone was a beautiful contraption that played musical records. My grand-daddy loved music, and he loved that old record player. He had quite a collection of all sorts of music."

"Aaahhh, that's nice! I would love a gramophone too!" the foxling said.

"Oh, you surely would. You would have loved your great great grandfox. Everyone loved him. Do you know why?" asked the old fox.

"Because he was the most kind and generous animal that anyone knew. He went out of his way to help everyone and anyone. Why I recall grandma getting upset because he came home soaked through his fur since he gave his umbrella to someone on the street so that they wouldn't get wet. One time he came home without his coat because he saw someone cold in the winter."

Grandpa fox slapped his knee to emphasize his point. "Can you imagine how much he cared for others?"

MOZART
RECORDS

"He sounds amazing grandpa," Felicity said. "He was, he was! Well, there came a day when a robber came into our den and stole my grand-daddy's favorite thing in the world!" Felicity's grandpa continued. "Not the gramophone!" Felicity gasped.

"Yes, you guessed it! His prized possession, the gramophone," grandpa nodded solemnly. "I found my grand-daddy sitting in this same rocking chair looking so sad. I was but a pup no bigger than you, and I felt so sad for him. So I went and sat on his lap and gave him a big hug and I said 'I'm sorry they took your record player, grand-daddy.' And do you know what he said to me?"

Felicity shook her head with her eyes wide open waiting for the answer.

"I'll never forget what he said to me. He said 'I'm just so sorry that he didn't take the records. What's the use of a gramophone without all the wonderful music that it plays.' Well I just opened my mouth in wonder. There he was sad for the robber instead of for himself!"

"Really, grandpa?" the foxling gasped.

"Honest to goodness! My grand-daddy was the most generous fox in the world. It was just the way he was. And that is why everyone loved and respected him so much. I remember him all the time, even though I'm old and grey around the muzzle. To this day I try to be like him, to be as great a fox as he was. Do you understand, Felicity, what I'm telling you?" he said kindly looking her in the eyes.

"I think so, grandpa" Felicity replied.
"Now what about your orange piece of chalk?" he asked.

The little foxling sat in quiet contemplation for a moment. Then she looked up at her grandpa and said, "You can't color the rainbow with just orange."
Her grandpa smiled and gave her a hug and kiss on the head. Felicity hugged him back, jumped off his lap and ran outside.

CHALK

She ran down the hill to the stream and found the rock by Wesley's den hole. Felicity opened her nap sack, took out the box of chalk and placed it on the rock. She stared at it a moment, sighed, and slowly walked back up the hill.

That afternoon after lunch came a knock at the door. Felicity opened it to find Wesley standing there smiling sheepishly. "Wesley?" the foxling exclaimed.

"Hi Felicity. I found your chalk, and I found this orange one out of the box too so I put it back in," he said handing it back to her. "Do you want to color some pictures together?" he asked shyly. "I would love to!" Felicity beamed.

CHALK

They ran down the hill to the stream
and spent the rest of the day gleefully
drawing on every stone, rock and tree
that they could find.

Felicity was engulfed in joy for she
didn't care about the chalk anymore,
so she was free to just have fun with
her friend.

CHALK

Written by Alia Einstein Diez
Illustrated by Shanti Ghosh
Graphic design by Sona Agarwal

www.sahajabooksforchildren.com

Book published by www.ingramspark.com